Dear Parent:

Buckle up! You are about to join your child on a very exciting journey. The destination? Independent reading!

Road to Reading will help you and your child get there. The program offers books at five levels, or Miles, that accompany children from their first attempts at reading to successfully reading on their own. Each Mile is paved with engaging stories and delightful artwork.

Getting Started
For children who know the alphabet and are eager to begin reading
• easy words • fun rhythms • big type • picture clues

Reading With Help
For children who recognize some words and sound out others with help
• short sentences • pattern stories • simple plotlines

Reading On Your Own
For children who are ready to read easy stories by themselves
• longer sentences • more complex plotlines • easy dialogue

First Chapter Books
For children who want to take the plunge into chapter books
• bite-size chapters • short paragraphs • full-color art

Chapter Books
For children who are comfortable reading independently
• longer chapters • occasional black-and-white illustrations

There's no need to hurry through the Miles. Road to Reading is designed without age or grade levels. Children can progress at their own speed, developing confidence and pride in their reading ability no matter what their age or grade.

So sit back and enjoy the ride—every Mile of the way!

To Jeff
L.H.B.

Library of Congress Cataloging-in-Publication Data
Hayward, Linda.
Pepe and Papa / by Linda Hayward ; illustrated by Laura Huliska-Beith.
   p. cm.—(Road to reading. Mile 1)
Summary: In this adaptation of a familiar story, a father and son take the advice of different people on how they should carry their chiles to market.
ISBN 0-307-26114-X (pbk.)—ISBN 0-307-46114-9 (GB)
[1. Folklore.] I. Huliska-Beith, Laura, ill. II. Title. III. Series.

PZ8.1.H3245 Pe 2001
398.2'0973'02—dc21
[E]   00-034775

A GOLDEN BOOK • New York
Golden Books Publishing Company, Inc. New York, New York 10106

ISBN: 0-307-26114-X (pbk)
ISBN: 0-307-46114-9 (GB)   A MMI

Pepe and Papa

by Linda Hayward
illustrated by Laura Huliska-Beith

Chiles on bushes.

Chiles in basket.

Basket on burro.

To market we go.

No, no!
Poor Pepe!

Chiles in basket.
Basket on Papa.

Pepe on burro.

To market we go.

No, no!
Poor Papa!

Chiles in basket.
Basket on Pepe.

Papa on burro.

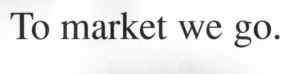

To market we go.

No, no!
Poor burro!

Chiles in basket.
Basket on burro.

Burro on Papa!

Papa in bushes.
Pepe in basket.

Chiles in burro.
Oh, oh!